Henry B. Thompson

Valkyrie III. vs. Defender

Official and signal program of the tenth contest for the emblem of

international supremacy, the America's cup

Henry B. Thompson

Valkyrie III. vs. Defender
Official and signal program of the tenth contest for the emblem of international supremacy, the America's cup

ISBN/EAN: 9783337427818

Printed in Europe, USA, Canada, Australia, Japan

Cover: Foto ©Andreas Hilbeck / pixelio.de

More available books at **www.hansebooks.com**

PRICE 10 CENTS.

VALKYRIE III.
VS
DEFENDER

ILLUSTRATED
OFFICIAL SIGNAL PROGRAMME AND
HAND-BOOK OF THE INTERNATIONAL YACHT RACES

FLAG OF
EARL OF DUNRAVEN
THE VALKYRIE'S SIGNAL.

FLAG OF
C. OLIVER ISELIN
THE DEFENDER'S SIGNAL.

FLAG OF
ROYAL YACHT SQUADRON.

FLAG OF THE
NEW YORK YACHT CLUB.

JAEGER, The Standard Underwear of the World!
Now at Greatly Reduced Prices!

Also ALL WOOL OUTING SHIRTS for YACHTING, FISHING,
BOATING, GOLFING, HUNTING, BICYCLING Etc.

B C D F G H J K L
M N P Q R S T V W

DR. JAEGER'S SANITARY WOOLEN SYSTEM CO.,
MAIN RETAIL STORE: 176 FIFTH AVE., Below 23RD ST.,   UP-TOWN BRANCH STORE: 1189 BROADWAY Near 28TH ST.,
DOWN-TOWN BRANCH STORE: 153 BROADWAY Below Cortlandt St.

VALKYRIE III vs. DEFENDER

Official and Signal Program of the Tenth Contest for the Emblem of International Supremacy

THE AMERICA'S CUP

CONTENTS

Compiled by
HENRY B. THOMPSON

Copyright, 1895, by Thompson & Thorp, Constable Building, Fifth Avenue and Eighteenth Street, New York.

Published by
EDWARD Y. THORP

BRITON VS. YANKEE

THE contest between Defender and Valkyrie III promises to be the hardest tussle for the America's cup since the gallant old Yankee schooner came sailing home forty-four years ago with brooms at her masthead, to show how she had swept the British seas. The crack yachts of two continents that are to contest for international honors more closely resemble each other in design than any two boats that have yet met in the series. Already the air is full of charges and counter charges of theft of principles and designs by the rival builders. In Defender's lines the Englishmen see only a clear appropriation of the British ideas, while Valkyrie's make Herreshoff's admirers declare that his designs have been boldly pirated.

Probably the fact is there has been an unwitting coming together of ideas due to the exigencies of the contest. Watson figured on building a boat to beat Vigilant, and Herreshoff tried to get a faster craft than the English Britannia. This mix up is undoubtedly due to Vigilant's visit last year to England, when she showed John Bull's boat builders the lines on which the Americans build their boats. So close are the races expected to be that neither side has "given away" any information that might be of advantage to the other side.

All efforts to "get a line" on either yacht have proven futile, for while both have been sailing neither has been raced as it will be when Yankee meets Briton.

If reports be true, the records of Valkyrie III are but times taken in luffing matches. It is also a matter of frequent observation that the Defender's managers were unwilling to show that yacht's best speed, as evidenced by their resorting to many extra tacks and sailing wide of the marks.

On Tuesday, September 3, the color of the hull of Valkyrie III was once more changed, so that as we go to press with this publication she is again all white. It is still a question with all except those directly interested in Valkyrie III whether the boats will be similar in this respect, or whether there will be the contrast in color that easily distinguishes them to the eye unfamiliar with their lines. The yachts will be easily recognized, however, by their signal flags displayed on the front cover of this program.

Sailing Directions

START.

The start will be made off Sandy Hook Lightship, the Preparatory Signal being given at 10.50 A.M. Starting Signal, 11 A.M.

COURSES.

No. 1. (Letter C.) From the starting line, to and around a mark fifteen miles to windward, or to leeward, and return, *leaving the mark on the starboard hand.*

No. 2. (Letter D.) From the starting line, ten miles to and around a mark; thence ten miles to and around a second mark; and thence ten miles to finish line, *turning the marks on the outside of the triangle, to port or starboard, according as the yachts are sent around.*

Starting and Finish Lines.—Will be between a point on the Committee Boat, indicated by a white flag, and the mainmast of the Lightship, or other Stakeboat if the start is made further out to sea. These lines will be at right angles with the outward and home courses, respectively.

Compass Courses.—Will be set before the Preliminary Signal is made. The Signals for Course No. 2 must be read beginning forward.

Marks.—Will be floats displaying a *red flag* with *white stripe.* The position of each float will be indicated by a tug showing a *red ball* and stationed about 100 yards beyond. Should a float be wrecked, its place will be taken by its marking tug, which will show the Club Signal in addition to the ball, and in turning the tug, the directions for turning the float will govern.

STARTING SIGNALS.

Preparatory.—A gun will be fired, the "Blue Peter" set, and a Red Ball hoisted.

Start.—Ten minutes later, a gun will be fired, and the ball will drop.

Handicap Time.—Two minutes later, a gun will be fired, and the "Blue Peter" hauled down.

Should a signal gun miss fire, a prolonged blast of the whistle will be given.

RECALL SIGNAL.

A yacht crossing the line before the Starting Signal is made will be recalled by a blast of the whistle and the display of her private signal.

[Continued on p. —]

DEFENDER

Description of Defender

FOR the first time the Yankee boat is the undersized craft. Americans had hoped Herreshoff would build a mountain of sails and spars, but the shrewd designer believed he had reached the limit of practicable sail area, and has sought speed in an easier driven body and finer lines without material decrease of sail. Her dimensions are: Length over all, 126 feet 6 inches; beam, 23 feet; draught, 19 feet; load water line, 90 feet. Her steel gaff is 65 feet, her steel boom 105, and mast from deck to hounds 92 feet. She is without doubt the most costly racing craft ever built. This fact doesn't bother her syndicate of wealthy yachtsmen, which is composed of W. K. Vanderbilt, Ex-Com. E. D. Morgan and C. Oliver Iselin. Her weight above the water line has been reduced by the use of manganese bronze and aluminum. Being ten per cent narrower than the challenger, and lighter, she needs less sail to drive her, and will have about 11,500 square feet, 1,000 less than Valkyrie. Defender cost fully $20,000 more than Vigilant. The contract price was $75,000, but with the changes and additional items the cost approaches $100,000. This great cost has come from the copper alloyed aluminum used in her upper body. Defender is totally unlike Vigilant in that she has no centerboard, but is an out and out keel boat. Her stability is due to her lightness above water, and her 35-foot lead bulb, weighing sixty tons. The total saving made by the use of aluminum is estimated at seven tons; the use of a hollow steel boom and steel gaff of tubular construction saves fully another ton. Defender is rigged in first-class style. Her hull could not be sounder. Her new mast is a magnificent spar. The steel work at the mast head is strong enough to resist the most savage of squalls. Her standing and running rigging are beyond praise. She is, in point of fact, quite competent to sail for a man's life.

Ex-Commodore James D. Smith, Chairman of the America's Cup Committee, voiced the general sentiment when he said: "I think Defender is the fastest boat America ever produced. Her work to windward is better than anything I have ever seen in my forty years' racing experience with boats and yachts. I am not much of a racing yachtsman nowadays, but there is nothing I like to see better than yacht races between two such crack flyers as the Defender and the challenging Valkyrie III. Of course I have not seen much of the Dunraven boat, but she promises to be the most dangerous contestant England has ever sent us to regain the cup."

Defender will be handled by a genuine Yankee crew from "down East," under Captain Hank Haff, and not as Vigilant was by a crew of all nations.

Defender's record is as follows:

July 20. Fifteen miles to leeward and return. Defender defeated Vigilant 2 minutes 45 seconds in 3 hours 18 minutes 40 seconds. Moderate wind at start, good whole sail breeze at end.

July 22. Thirty miles, triangular course. Defender defeated Vigilant 9 minutes 17 seconds in 4 hours 19 minutes 30 seconds; light variable winds.

July 29. Twenty-one miles, Long Island Sound. Defender defeated Vigilant 1 minute 49 seconds, in 2 hours 55 minutes 32 seconds; very light breeze at start, moderate at finish.

July 30. Sixty-four miles, Hempstead to New London. Defender broke down three miles from the finish when leading Vigilant about three minutes. The wind was twenty miles an hour all the time and Vigilant sailed the course in 4 hours 40 minutes 37 seconds.

July 31. Thirty-six miles, New London to Newport. Defender

PILOTS

CAPTAINS

HELMSMEN

BE FAIR!

GIVE THE GREAT YACHTS SEA ROOM!

Don't pass the yachts to the windward!

Give them a wide lee and try not to give them your steamer's wash!

There is room on the broad Atlantic for every steamer attending the races without repeating the annoyances of two years ago!

Let all officers in charge of steamers be jealous of their country's reputation for fair play, and bound in honor to give both contestants all the sea room they need, and there will probably be little complaint.

[Continued from page 3.]

defeated Vigilant 12 minutes 2 seconds, in 4 hours 6 minutes 10 seconds. The wind was about twelve knots an hour.

August 2. Thirty miles, triangular course, Goelet cups. Defender broke down when six miles from the finish, and was leading Vigilant about eleven minutes. Fresh breeze.

August 3. Thirty-seven miles, Newport to Vineyard Haven. Defender defeated Vigilant 6 minutes 24 seconds, in 3 hours 11 minutes 34 seconds. Fresh ten-knot breeze all the way.

August 5. Thirty-seven miles, Vineyard Haven to Newport. Defender defeated Vigilant 9 minutes 9 seconds, in 4 hours 9 minutes. Ten-knot breeze all the way.

August 6. Twenty-one miles, triangular course, Defender defeated Vigilant 6 minutes 10 seconds, in 2 hours 44 minutes 18 seconds. Light and varying breezes.

August 8. Twenty-one miles, triangular course, Defender defeated Jubilee 9 minutes 19 seconds, in 2 hours 16 minutes 15 seconds. Light and variable winds.

August 20. Forty miles. Defender withdrew after completing first twenty miles. She was then 4 minutes and 3 seconds ahead of Vigilant in 2 hours 17 minutes 36 seconds. Wind about twelve knots.

August 29. Twenty-four miles, triangular course. Defender defeated Vigilant 18 minutes 3 seconds, in 4 hours 49 minutes 40 seconds. A drifting match on the first leg, light breeze on second leg, and good breeze on last leg.

August 30. Twenty miles. Defender defeated Vigilant 5 minutes 12 seconds, in 2 hours 52 minutes 10 seconds. Wind ten knots an hour.

[*Program—Continued from page 1*]

POSTPONEMENT SIGNALS, Etc.

Letter H.—Do you assent to postponing start until later in
the day?

Letter G. Do you assent to calling race off for the day ?

If a yacht assents she will display Letter C.

If a yacht dissents she will display Letter D.

Race postponed on account of fog, Letter L.

Race postponed until later in the day, Letter S.

Race postponed until another day, Letter Z.

Letter V.—The starting point will be shifted out from the
Lightship.

In case of serious accident to either yacht, prior to the Preparatory Signal, she will display Letter M, and shall have
sufficient time to repair before being required to start. Should
such accident occur during a race, she shall have sufficient time
to repair before being required to start in the next race.

In case the start is postponed, or the starting point is shifted
from the Lightship, a Preliminary Signal will be made by firing
a gun and displaying the Yacht Ensign at the fore.

The Committee Boat will display the Club signal at the fore,
and the Committee flag aft.

Should the Committee Boat fail to reach the finish, her place
will be taken by a vessel displaying a red ball.

S. NICHOLSON KANE,

CHESTER GRISWOLD, ⎬ Regatta Committee.

IRVING GRINNELL,

The Racing Rules, Time Allowance, and System of Measurement of the New York Yacht Club shall govern.

Best three out of five races, outside of headlands, over
courses each thirty nautical miles in length, and with a time limit
of six hours.

The first, third and fifth races shall be to windward or to leeward and return. The second and fourth races shall be around an
equilateral triangle, one leg; and the first, if the wind permits,
being to windward.

One day shall intervene between each racing day, unless by
special agreement. A race postponed or not finished within the
time limit shall be decided before the next race in the series is
taken up.

The races will be started off Sandy Hook Lightship, the Preparatory Signal being made at 11:30 ... but if on the day of a
race to windward or leeward the ... unable to hold ... the
Lightship, then the race will be started ... point further
on, toward

VALKYRIE III

Description of Valkyrie III

VALKYRIE III is 129 feet over all, with 26 feet 2 inches beam, 20 feet draught, and has 77 tons of lead in her keel. Her water line measurement is about 90 feet. She is built from lines laid down by G. L. Watson, England's foremost naval architect and designer of the Thistle, Valkyrie II, Queen Mab and a host of equally well-known yachts. Valkyrie, like Defender, is syndicate built, despite the fact that she is always referred to as Lord Dunraven's boat. Her syndicate is composed of the Earl of Dunraven, Earl of Lonsdale, Emperor William's chum ; Lord Wolverton, and Harry McCalmont, called the "wealthiest commoner of England." Roughly speaking, she is a flat, shallow boat, with a deep fin keel, and relies like Defender on the enormous amount of lead placed very low down for power. She has a tremendous overhang and a great sheer. Viewed as a whole, she might be called a modified composite fin keel cutter of great beam and enormous sail power. She is the ninth vessel built expressly to capture the America's Cup. Her sail spread is the largest ever carried on a single sticker, and though it is not definitely known just what she will throw to the breeze in the races, it will be about 12,500 square feet of duck. Her mast from deck to head measures 96 feet. The gaff is 59 feet long, and her main boom is 105 feet, and like the Defender's is made of steel, combining great strength with a saving of weight when compared with the usual wooden boom.

As this publication goes to press before the official figures are announced, the above are given as approximately correct.

Valkyrie III was built especially for the light winds which prevail off here during the fall. In light winds she is a decidedly superior boat to Britannia, which so signally defeated Vigilant, but in heavy weather she showed such instability that there was a hasty addition of from twelve to fifteen tons of outside lead on her keel. Unless she was purposely held back in her trial races in England, to keep the Yankees from "getting a line on her," she may not, after all, be a better boat than the Britannia. In fact, there has been somewhat of a public demand across the water that the Prince of Wales' sturdy cutter be sent over here. Valkyrie's trials were not satisfactory.

The Valkyrie's crew are all Englishmen, Capt. William Cranfield will divide honors at the helm with Capt. Sycamore.

The record of Valkyrie III is as follows :

July 1. Defeated Britannia by 46 seconds in drift, but beaten by Britannia 1 minute 18 seconds on time allowance. The race was at fifty miles, the course being sailed over three times, but was declared finished at the end of the second round, the distance sailed being thirty-eight miles. Half a mile from the finish Valkyrie III led by five miles, but ran into a calm. Britannia came along under a light breeze, and when Valkyrie III got it they were on level terms. In the half mile her gain was 46 seconds.

July 3. Britannia defeated Valkyrie III. 3 minutes 8 seconds, actual time, and Ailsa 1 minute 10 seconds, in a fifty-mile race. The wind was strong and Valkyrie III did not attempt to carry all her sail.

July 5. Valkyrie III defeated Ailsa in a fresh breeze in a race lasting 2 hours and 15 minutes, by 15 minutes. Britannia did not start.

July 6. Valkyrie III defeated Britannia 18 minutes 26 seconds, and Ailsa 19 minutes 47 seconds, in a fifty-mile race. The beating was greater than that, for the other two crossed the line too soon, and Valkyrie III waited for them to come up. The breeze was about twelve knots an hour.

C. OLIVER ISELIN

E. D. MORGAN

W. K. VANDERBILT

THE SYNDICATE OWNERS OF "DÉFENDER"

(By courtesy of "Leslie's Weekly")

C. Oliver Iselin

VERY few of the thousands of persons who have been reading about the great American sloop Defender realize what a great amount of brain-work has been expended in the preparation of the yacht for the great marine battle beginning next Saturday.

The yachtsmen who furnished the money with which to build Defender are William K. Vanderbilt, Edwin D. Morgan, and C. Oliver Iselin. The first two named asked Mr. Iselin to undertake the management and fitting out of the yacht from the time she was delivered by her builders until the international races were sailed. This was a work of the greatest importance, and members of the New York Yacht Club are loud in their praise of Mr. Iselin for the way in which he has performed it.

On January 17 the New York Yacht Club officially announced the names of the men who had agreed to build a cup defender. Five days later the contract was signed with the Herreshoff's to construct the yacht. She was to be delivered by June 15, but owing to delays in obtaining aluminum plates and other material, it was 158 days before she was launched, and a week later she was formally accepted by her owners.

Subtracting twenty-two Sundays from the total number of days, it took just 136 working days to construct Defender. Much of Mr. Iselin's time and advice was needed during these days of construction, and nearly all the rest of his time was spent in drilling the crew of Deer Island sailors on board Colonia, the sloop that was chartered for the purpose of breaking them in, as it were, for the more serious work ahead.

When Defender was launched on June 29 the real work began for Mr. Iselin. The three days during which the yacht remained fast on the ways were anxious days for him. From her launching date until she was officially selected to defend the cup, sixty-two days elapsed. Of these, three were spent in the Bristol ways, there were nine Sundays, and she has sailed in twelve races, leaving only thirty-eight actual working days that they have had to get her into shape for what will undoubtedly be the greatest contest ever witnessed between two single-stick yachts.

It is no wonder, then, that yachtsmen who know these facts in a general way are talking as much of C. Oliver Iselin as of the great white sloop. Mr. Iselin was born in this city about forty-one years ago. He is the son of Adrian Iselin, the banker. He received a liberal education at home and abroad, and at an early age developed a fondness for yachting. One of his earliest yachts was the famous jib and mainsail open boat Mary Emma, built for him by Pat McGlehan of Pamrapo, N. J. Many a race he won with her. His next boat, the open sloop Dare Devil, was built by Jake Schmidt, of Stapleton, S. I. It was at the tiller of such boats as these that many a smart racing skipper of to-day took his first lesson.

In May, 1887, Mr. Iselin's steel sloop Titania—a seventy-footer—was launched from the Piepgras yard at City Island. She was designed for him by the late Edward Burgess. Her speed and seaworthy qualities were so good that the Auchincloss Bros. commissioned A. Cary Smith to design a boat of the same water-line measurement to beat her. The Katrina, now owned by George Work, was the result. The rivalry was keen between these two boats for years, until the late Robert W. Inman bought the Titania and converted her into a schooner. She is now called the Dagmar. Titania, under Capt. Iselin's skillful handling, won many a race, among them the Goelet Cup for sloops in 1889.

Mr. Iselin's first wife was Miss Fanny Garner, a niece of Commodore Garner, who was lost in the steamer Mohawk in 1876. She died about six years ago, leaving four children. During the spring and summer of 1893 Mr. Iselin had charge of Vigilant, and prepared her for the races against Lord Dunraven's Valkyrie II. His work at that time was so thoroughly appreciated that the New York Yacht Club presented him with a handsome cup for his services.

In June, 1894, Mr. Iselin married Miss Hope Goddard, the only daughter of Col. William Goddard, of Providence. She is said to be an heiress with twenty millions at her command. Mrs. Iselin christened Defender when she was launched, and she has lived on the yacht and sailed on her in every race since the launching. She takes a deep interest in Defender, and naturally in everything that her clever and accomplished husband does.

Mr. Iselin sailed on Vigilant in several of her important races in British waters last year, he having visited Norway and other points of interest shortly after his marriage.

Mr. Iselin's work on Defender is so fresh in the minds of all American yachtsmen that it needs no rehearsal. It is doubtful if there could have been found another man who would have so unselfishly devoted his time and money to the object in view, and who could have accomplished so much in the short time allotted to him.

The crew of Defender admire and respect Mr. Iselin, and they take a personal interest in the work done on board the big sloop. All feel that she is bound to win, and every man Jack of them means to obey orders to the letter and try his level best to make her win.

No man ever worked harder to bring his boat to the post in true racing form than has Mr. Iselin. He has lost sleep fretting about the Defender, and all through the struggles and breakdowns he has held his courage. He has tremendous staying powers, and is just the man to be at the head. There is not a bit of the quitter in his makeup, and now that race day is near at hand, he should receive the full sympathy and support of his countrymen.

SCHOONER YACHT "AMERICA"
First Winner of the Famous Cup

All of the details of each day's program will be found in this complete handbook.

ILLUSTRATION.

When the committee boat displays code flags refer to our front cover and find what letters the flags represent. Then to general program for meaning of single flags, and to the following for flags displayed in sets of three. See compass and chart pages for further explanation.

SIGNAL CODE FLAGS USED.   COURSES SIGNALED.

D R C	North.
D B F	N. ½ E.
D B G	N. by E.
D B H	N. by E. ½ E.
D B J	N. N. E.
D B K	N. N. E. ½ E.
D B L	N. E. by N.
D B M	N. E. ½ N.
D B N	N. E
D B P	N. E. ½ E.
D B Q	N. E. by E.
D B R	N. E. by E. ½ E.
D B S	E. N. E.
D B T	E. N. E. ½ E.
D B V	E. by N.
D B W	E. ½ N.
D C B	East.
D C F	E. ½ S.
D C G	E. by S.
D C H	E. by S. ½ S.
D C J	E. S. E.
D C K	S. E. by E. ½ E.
D C L	S. E. by E.
D C M	S. E. ½ E.
D C N	S. E.
D C P	S. E. ½ S.
D C Q	S. E. by S.
D C R	S. S. E. ½ E.
D C S	S. S. E.
D C T	S. by E. ½ E.
D C V	S. by E.
D C W	S. ½ E.
D F B	South.
D F C	S. ½ W.
D F G	S. by W.
D F H	S. by W. ½ W.
D F J	S. S. W.
D F P	S. S. W. ½ W.
D F K	S. W. by S.
D F L	S. W. ½ S.
D F M	S. W.
D F N	S. W. ½ W.
D F Q	S. W. by W.
D F R	S. W. by W. ½ W.
D F S	W. S. W.
D F T	W. by S. ½ S.
D F V	W. by S.
D F W	W. ½ S.
D G B	West.
D G C	W. ½ N.
D G F	W. by N.
D G H	W. N. W. ½ W.
D G J	W. N. W.
D G K	N. W. by W. ½ W.
D G L	N. W. by W.
D G M	N. W. ½ W.
D G N	N. W.
D G P	N. W. ½ W.
D G Q	N. W. by N.
D G R	N. N. W. ½ W.
D G S	N. N. W.
D G T	N. by W. ½ W.
D G V	N. by W.
D G W	N. ½ W.

PURITAN

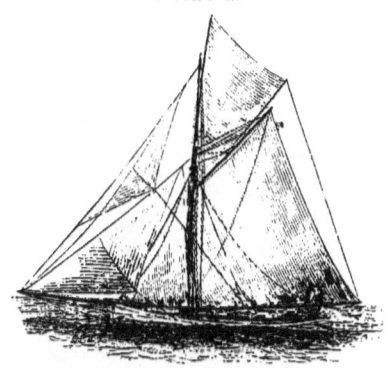

TEN years ago, September 7, 1885, Puritan and Genesta made five attempts before a finish was made within a time limit, one of these postponements being caused by a foul. Puritan finally won by 16 minutes 19 seconds in light winds on September 14th. In a race of twenty miles to windward and return on September 16th, Genesta was accommodated with many kinds of "cutter weather," but was not equal to the first Burgess cup defender. A grand race was sailed, and resulted in a victory of 1 minute 38 seconds for the Puritan. The late Robert Center, one of America's foremost yachtsmen, was aboard the Genesta as the cup committee's representative.

Puritan was a revelation to all Americans. She made new records for all her points of excellence. She pointed closer and footed faster than any yacht had done before, and her designer was at once recognized as leader in all American ideas on yacht designing.

Puritan's dimensions were: Length overall, 93 feet; length water line, 81 feet 1½ inches; beam, 22 feet 7 inches; draught, 8 feet 5 inches. Her gaff was 47 feet long, and her boom 76 feet long—each being about seventy per cent of the gaff and boom of Defender.

Lord Dunraven and the English Syndicate

CLIPPINGS FROM THE PRESS

LORD DUNRAVEN needs no introduction to American readers. He is a man of varied attainments, and a sportsman of the best type. He takes defeat gracefully; he wears the honors of victory moderately; he never puts on airs, and the one thing that would make life unendurable to him would be idleness, and he is going to keep on trying for the cup until he gets it, or gets too old to try any longer.

Lord Lonsdale, Lord Wolverton and Mr. Harry L. B. McCalmont will share the pecuniary burden with him.

Commodore Smith, in speaking of the Cup Committee's conference with Lord Dunraven at the New York Yacht Club house, said:

"Remarkable accord and unanimity were displayed between the parties at this meeting. Only the preliminary conditions of the cup races were to be agreed upon, and Lord Dunraven assented to the conditions which we had mapped out as proper, and, in fact, even suggested certain things which we had always hitherto believed desirable."

"Anything for sport" might well be the motto of Hugh Cecil Lowther, fifth Earl of Lonsdale. To the robust constitution of the outdoor-loving Englishman he unites the restless energy of a "down East" Yankee. Born rich and in a prosaic age, he has eschewed all temptations to lead a life of slothful ease, and, in his way, has contrived to make life exceedingly interesting.

He started for the North Pole by way of Canada. Just how near he got to it nobody knows exactly, but he stuck to it much longer than was pleasant for his attendants, who would have much preferred warning their shins before a comfortable log fire.

Before that he had exhausted the excitement of shooting big game in the Rocky Mountains—a trip, by the way, on which his wife, Lady Grace Lowther, also was then, accompanied him. "She," to quote from an English journal, which, to tell the truth, can hardly be regarded as an authority on the subject of bears, "cooked the food, and, quite as courageous as he, held the ponies while he shot the grizzlies, the huge beasts often passing so near her that the animals shivered with fright. But she never trembled."

Lonsdale is an all-round sportsman. He has a temperament that keeps him on the go. Motion seems to be to him what rest is to other persons. Perhaps this is why the Emperor of Germany is so fond of him, having a temperament of the same sort. His recent lavish entertainment of the Kaiser has been described in cable dispatches. It is said to have cost him a small fortune, but a small fortune makes a very small hole in his long purse.

The quality of the sporting blood that is in Lonsdale was shown when, just before the yachting season opened in British waters, hearing that Howard Gould was going to race the Herreshoff twenty-rater Niagara against all comers, he got rid of his Deidre and commissioned young Fife to build an up-to-date fin-keel yacht of the same class—that is, about forty-six feet on the water line—

for the express purpose of beating the Yankee craft, if possible. The boat was rushed through in a few weeks, and to that British critics have, in a measure, attributed her failure to accomplish what had been expected of her. She is a fast boat, but not quite fast enough to catch the Niagara.

Like most Englishmen who go in for yachting, Lord Lonsdale is not content with one boat. For cruising purposes he has a large schooner, the Verena, of 316 tons, Thames measurement. She isn't speedy, but she is fitted up with everything necessary to make life afloat enjoyable. It was on board of her at Cowes last year that Lord Lonsdale entertained the Emperor of Germany and won his royal favor. The Prince of Wales was one of the guests.

Lord Lonsdale was born in 1857, and married in 1878 Lady Grace Gordon, sister of the present Marquis of Huntley. He succeeded to his title in 1882.

Lord Wolverton, another titled member of the Valkyrie syndicate, is accounted one of the luckiest men in England, though what was luck to him was death to others. His natal day, September 24, 1864, dawned upon the second son of a fourth son. Five years later his grandfather was created first Lord Wolverton, and between then and 1888 the lives which barred his way to the peerage and one of the largest fortunes of the world succumbed to the decrees of fate, and Frederick Glyn inherited a coronet, and not only a balance in the bank, a balance which went well into seven figures, pounds sterling, but a bank of his own in which to deposit it. He is head of the firm of Glyn, Mills, Currie & Co., whose establishment in Lombard Street, London, is synonymous with "Tom Tiddler's ground," where those who have the "entrée" can pick up as much gold as they please.

Mr. McCalmont is the only member of the syndicate who hasn't a title. But he has a mint of money, has recently been elected a member of Parliament—which fact, it is said, will prevent him from coming over to see the races for the cup—and enjoys the distinction of owning the finest and speediest seagoing steam yacht in the world, the Giralda. She is so constructed that in case of war, quick-firing guns could be mounted upon her and she could be utilized as a commerce destroyer, for which her great speed would render her admirably adapted. And her owner has patriotically announced that if England ever wants her for that purpose England can have her. But for the present, life on board of her savors of anything rather than the rigors and hardships of naval service. That may be inferred from the fact that on her muster roll are five cooks and about half a dozen stewards.

All the members of the syndicate are sportsmen, and rich enough to stick to the game of building cup challengers or cup defenders almost as long as those who have invested in the latest Herreshoff creation.

Two English Cup Challengers

GALATEA, 1886

VALKYRIE, 1893

HERRESHOFF

THE Herreshoffs of Bristol, R. I., father and son, are the most famous small boat builders in America, and into Defender put the experience of years with the building of other cup defenders.

Herreshoff has demonstrated his capability to turn out a boat of the keel form far superior in all the true characteristics of a racing yacht to those of the cup victor of 1893.

Has Watson enough skill or experience to beat Herreshoff at his own game? When we look at Gloriana and Wasp, two splendid keel craft, or at Vigilant, a magnificent centerboard boat; at Niagara, a fin-keel vessel—all of which have demonstrated their superiority, at one time or another, to all antagonists, the presumption is that Nat Herreshoff's star is in the ascendant and that Dunraven's new craft will be defeated.

To build a successful cup defender is the ambition of every designer. The wonderful success of three Burgess boats so completely satisfied the English yachtsmen that they did not again attempt to wrest the honors from the Yankees until 1893. They could not beat a Burgess, and with one victory already scored and another well in hand, Mr. Herreshoff has shown himself able to cope with the many difficult problems that all lead to success if solved or defeat if not mastered. The careful analysis Mr. Watson is making of "everything in sight" about Defender is evidence of the high regard he has for the prowess of the Yankee.

MAGIC

VAL-KI'-REE

To the Editor of The Sun.

SIR: Will you give the correct pronunciation, origin, and definition of the word Valkyrie?　　T. S.

NEW YORK, August 30.

The name of Lord Dunraven's yacht is pronounced Val-ki-ree, with the accent on the second syllable. The word signifies "chooser of the slain." It comes from the Icelandic Valkyrja, more familiar in the German form, Walküre. In the Norse mythology it means one of the virgin attendants of Odin, who carry to Valhalla heroes slain in battle.—The Sun.

IN CHINESE WATERS

OPEN TO CHALLENGE IN THE FIJI ISLANDS

Defender and Valkyrie III Compared

By A. G. McVEY

IN

New York Herald, August 26th, 1895.

In a Moderate Breeze a Toss Up, with Defender's Chances Good.

VALKYRIE III IS DANGEROUS.

She May Develop Elements of Strength Which It Is Impossible Now to Forecast.

DEFENDER'S CREW IS RAW.

Much Depends on the Start and Not a Little on the Handling of the Boats.

I have no use for letter writers who send communications to the managing editor, saying, "Why don't your yachting man give us his 'private opinion' of the coming races?" "Private opinion" is funny, indeed, for I have not got any to give. All that I have ever written about the Valkyrie and the Defender has been in accord with the best light in me, let the axe fall where it would. In nothing is it so hard to prophesy as the result of a yacht race. What may appear all right to-day may be all wrong to-morrow, for in yacht racing there is a constant change going on of wind, chance and weather, and with the fight for champion honors narrowing closer every day, a boat has to be built almost for the weather of the country she is to race in. Ten years ago you yachtsmen were just getting an idea of design and equipment. The problems of design, of power and of sail were but little understood, and men were then in the dark, because they were not able to grasp questions which since have been solved by building.

For instance, Americans generally knew but little of the cutter rig except, perhaps, such as was learned from the British boats Maggie, Stranger, Madge, and others of the earlier cutters. To-day nearly all the young amateurs ... and young John Paine, of Boston, has seen the British them better, for he has invented some new boat men ... far better than Watson's. ... matches for the cup is under taking a profounder study ... much more of the construction ...

THE LAYMAN PNEUMATIC SPORTING AND OUTING BOAT

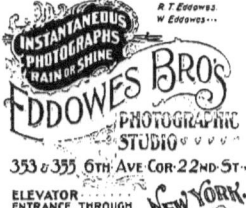

SCORE CARD.

	Start	1st Mark	2d Mark	Finish	Elapsed Time	Corrected Time
DEFENDER 1st Day. VALKYRIE						
DEFENDER 2d Day. VALKYRIE						
DEFENDER 3d Day VALKYRIE						
DEFENDER 4th Day. VALKYRIE						
DEFENDER 5th Day. VALKYRIE						

The times will be bulletined in large figures on the Committee Boat. This feature of the International Races is new and will be greatly appreciated by the public.

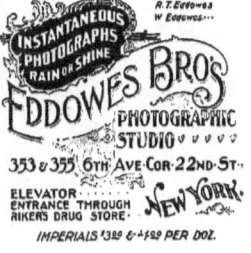

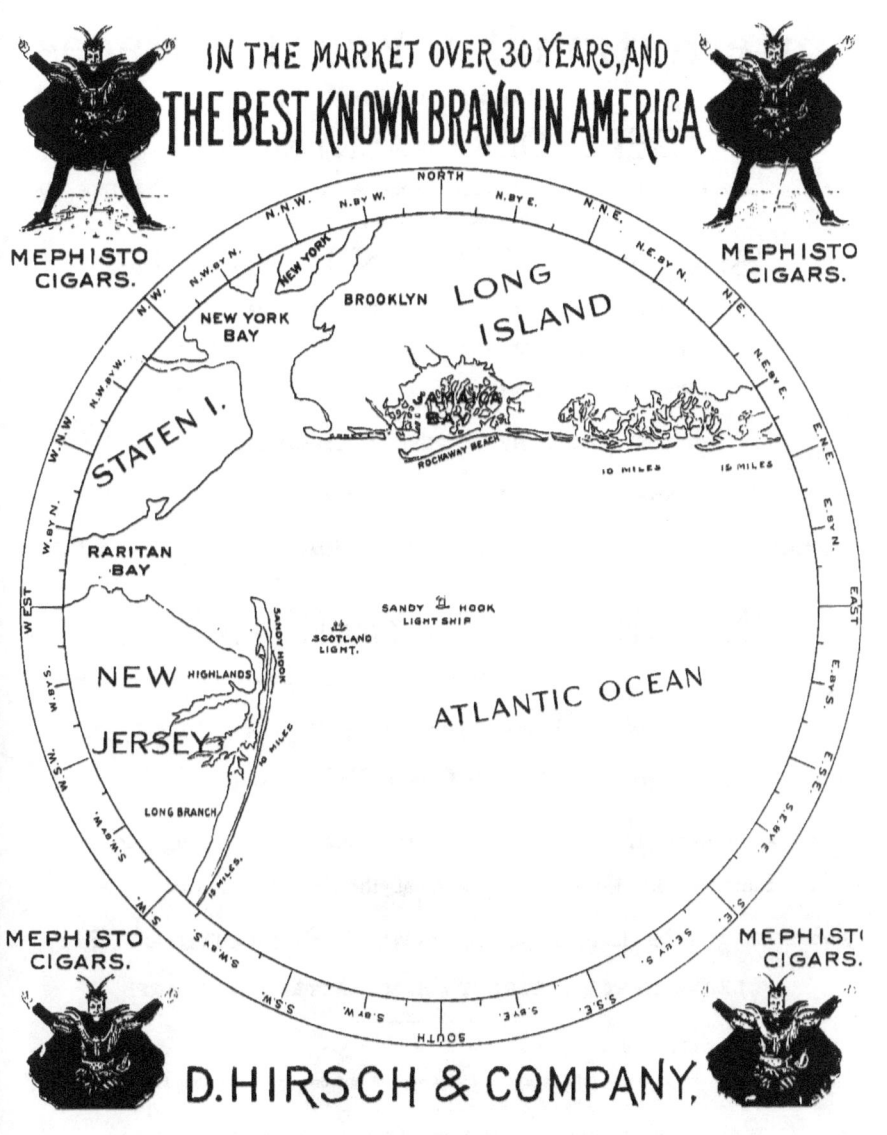

IN THE MARKET OVER 30 YEARS, AND
THE BEST KNOWN BRAND IN AMERICA

MEPHISTO CIGARS.

MEPHISTO CIGARS.

MEPHISTO CIGARS.

MEPHISTO CIGARS.

D. HIRSCH & COMPANY,

International : Yacht : Races

⊷≈ 1895 ≈⊶

DEFENDER—VALKYRIE III.

An unusual opportunity to witness the Races for the **AMERICA'S CUP** will be afforded a limited number of persons on the

Steamer "MOUNT HOPE"

Of the FALL RIVER AND PROVIDENCE STEAMBOAT CO.

She will leave Pier 18, North River, foot of Murray Street, at 9.30 A. M.

And accompany the contesting yachts over the course each day.

MUSIC BY A FINE ORCHESTRA.

Refreshments will be served by a First-class Caterer.

$3.00 - - **FARE FOR EACH RACE** - - **$3.00**

INTERNATIONAL YACHT RACES.

The Seagoing Twin Screw Steel Steamer

⊷≈ "AL FOSTER," ≈⊶

will accompany the Yachts over entire course, fast enough to be at The Start, at the Outer Marks and at the Finish for the

America's Cup, Saturday. September 7th,

LEAVE EAST 31st STREET 9 A. M., BATTERY 9.45 SHARP.

TICKETS, Limited, - - - **$2.00 EACH.**

For Sale at Tyson's Principal Hotels, Cook's, 261 and 1225 Broadway, and Battery Pier.

We would request our Patrons to board the Steamer at 31st Street, to avoid delay at the Battery.

[*Defender and Valkyrie III Compared—Continued.*]

a naval architect some question, and he could not answer it. For instance, Watson might be asked why 26 feet 2 inches extreme beam is better than 25 feet 11 inches, and, again, he might be asked why 15 feet across the taffrail is not better than 10 feet. So it goes. Question after question might be asked of yacht architects, and to none of them, when it comes down to a few inches, especially in beam, can any of them give a satisfactory answer. When such easy questions as the above cause a bit of trouble for them, can it be wondered at I most reluctantly approach the task laid before me—with great anxiety, apprehension, yes, fear—lest time may prove all my predictions a sort of dreamy imagination? Before proceeding to compare the Defender with the Valkyrie, I ask myself this simple question : " How much is the Vigilant faster than she was in 1893?"

VIGILANT IS IMPROVED.

On my own question I'm brought up with a round turn, and " Where am I at? " suggests itself. Some inquisitive reader shouts out to himself, " How does he know anything about it? "

Then, again, comes the question : " Is she improved at all ? "

In answer to the first question : " Is she improved this year over 1893?" I say, emphatically, yes; and why? Having the data of Vigilant before me as she was in 1893 and as she is to-day, an intelligent comparison can be made of her, because of the dealing with a known quantity.

How is she improved?

In two ways, at least.

First, the Vigilant is not now fenced in with a fixed water line length of 87.60 feet. In 1893 this was the dead-line mark for her. It meant positive disqualification, because the New York Yacht Club and Lord Dunraven agreed that either ship going anything over two per cent. over 85 feet water line should be disqualified, hence the Vigilant lacked the needed power to properly carry her sail well, stand up on her feet and present her lateral plane for best effect for side pressure, because she could take in no ballast. In other words, the Vigilant in 1893 could not of herself exert enough power to carry her sail properly in all conditions of wind and weather.

How is she now in this latter respect?

The 87.60 feet water line fence has been taken down, and under the terms of the present match the Vigilant can go up to 90 feet water line before the bar of disqualification has been reached. This is an advantage, and it carries with it—what?

NOW THE BRITANNIA.

Through with Vigilant brings me to Britannia, the ever lucky, splendidly sailed and well handled ship. Nor must Lord Dunraven's sunken Valkyrie II be left out of the comparison. I have never spoken through the columns of this great international newspaper or given my opinion of Valkyrie II as compared with the Britannia. Now that I am sizing up the Vigilant for comparison with Defender and Valkyrie, it is quite necessary for me to tell the reason why Valkyrie II, to my mind, was a better boat than the Britannia. The Vigilant over the cup courses, outside a hammer in a steep sea and wind, was quite eight minutes faster than the Valkyrie II in 1893, as an all-around boat. I never believed, all things else being even, that the Britannia was the equal of the Valkyrie II. Yacht racing records are uncertain. They do not size up the performances of the boats on the level.

A boat which goes through a season like Niagara with a big

[*Continued on page 19.*]

MAYFLOWER

THE cup-defending Boston yachtsmen were so elated over the victory of Messrs. Forbes and Burgess with the Puritan that when Lieutenant Henn challenged for the cup in 1886 with his yacht Galatea, General Charles J. Paine ordered of Mr. Burgess another sloop which would be an enlarged Puritan.

The genius of Burgess was triumphant. Mayflower was a trifle superior to Puritan in that grandest test of a racing machine—a thresh to windward in a whole-sail breeze, when the spray comes a-dashing over the weather bow and wets the helmsman's face. Mayflower was indeed superb.

The Galatea was a disappointment to everybody, being inferior to Mayflower, Puritan and Genesta. In the second race, on September 11th, that best of all breezes, a full northwester, gave the contestants ample power for a great race, but the English yacht was not " up to snuff," and Mayflower won in splendid style eleven minutes ahead.

EARL OF DUNRAVEN
Challenger for the America's Cup

[*Defender and Valkyrie III Compared—Continued.*]

winning per cent on its merits shows that she is fast. But with Britannia it was partly luck, partly good handling, and long service of the skipper and crew on board the same ship. The Vigilant had many a race on the other side in hand against the Britannia, when she lost it by a fluke. In light winds the Britannia showed up a shade faster than the Vigilant. In a good, whole-sail breeze, on open courses, such as was had off Bangor, Kingston and Queenstown, Ireland, the Vigilant, when she was not handicapped by staying so often, always led the Britannia. To get at the facts of Vigilant's racing with the Valkyrie and Britannia in British waters, I asked "Lun" Miller, formerly mate of the Jubilee, also second mate of Vigilant when she was in England, and now mate of Vigilant, how he sized up the Britannia and the Valkyrie II with the Vigilant. He told me, just in such weather as we had in the last cup race, that the Britannia never did nearly as well with Vigilant as Valkyrie II did. Said Miller, "I'm sure Valkyrie II was faster than Britannia."

The Valkyrie II's sailing with Britannia before she came over here clearly showed that she was just a bit better boat than the Britannia. I have always thought, and still think, that on the level the Vigilant in 1893 was at least six minutes faster than the Britannia, and that she was more rather than under. Any one can dispute this proposition, but it seems to me that the sailing of the two ships clearly proves it. This brings me then to Britannia and Vigilant of to-day, and how each sizes up as against the other.

Is Britannia faster than she was in 1894?

She has a larger sail plan, and surely Carter has not been on her three seasons without being able to improve her. Certain minor alterations have been made on the Britannia, but they are not so radical as those made on the Vigilant, so a fair margin for the improvement on the former would be, say, two to three minutes faster than she was in 1894. Allowing, then, that Vigilant is improved five minutes, and to-day, over our cup courses, she is at least seven or eight minutes faster than the Britannia, then how do Defender and Valkyrie size up on a line drawn through Britannia and Vigilant?

VALKYRIE III AND VIGILANT.

Taking Valkyrie III and comparing her with Vigilant—for the latter craft is surely the boat to size her up by—and what does one find? There are some things about Valkyrie and Vigilant which are not conundrums, but facts, and, having certain facts, some questions anent these two ships can well be dealt with.

On the displacement question there is a difference of about ten tons between Defender and Valkyrie, the American boat having the smaller displacement. This is just so much less weight to force and drive through the water. Again, on the question of wetted surface, an all-important factor in yacht racing: Now that Valkyrie has been sunk by weight and taken on more draught, being, according to well-informed parties, something over twenty feet draught, the Valkyrie has more wetted surface than the Defender, certainly an advantage for the Yankee ship.

On the question of sail spread, the plan of the Defender has been changed, chiefly and solely because designer Herreshoff found out after the Defender was overboard that she could carry more canvas; also, because the same designer first learned through these columns that the Valkyrie had a steel boom 105 feet 6 inches long. So far as is known, Watson put a big suit of canvas on the Valkyrie

[*Continued on page 31.*]

VIGILANT

A ROUND this great sloop there cluster so many pleasant memories of her work that there are many people loth to give her second place in their affections.

The Iselin-Morgan syndicate, who built the Vigilant, was composed of the largest body of representative yachtsmen ever organized for a similar investment. It consisted of Messrs. C. Oliver Iselin, Com. E. D. Morgan, August Belmont, Oliver H. P. Belmont, Perry Belmont, Cornelius Vanderbilt, Charles R. Flint, Chester W. Chapin, George C. Clark, Dr. W. Barton Hopkins, E. M. Fulton, and the estate of W. Astor Carey.

The Vigilant's dimensions were: Length over all, 130 feet; water line, 85 feet (afterward increased by additional ballast); beam, 26 feet; draught, 14 feet. Her centerboard is 16 feet long, and it drops 10 feet.

Vigilant's records were:

October 7, 1893, won by 5 min. 48 sec. October 9, 1893, won by 10 min. 35 sec. October 13, 1893, won by 40 sec.

There is little doubt but that Valkyrie's misfortune on the 13th of October has in a measure contributed to Lord Dunraven's determination to win the cup.

Nathaniel G. Herreshoff did his best with Vigilant. Designed expressly for racing in the waters off Sandy Hook, to defend the America's cup, with only a few turns, she was indeed great. She did the trick. It is always wise to judge by results. Vigilant fulfilled her destiny—that of a cup defender.

Her designer's ambition to build a cup defender was realized, and the experience gained in the races of 1893 undoubtedly pointed in the direction of deeper keels and less beam. The Colonia's work, compared with Vigilant, pointed to that conclusion, and the Valkyrie's wonderful windward work on October 13, 1893, confirmed it.

In Vigilant's races this year we find that the foundations for a new type of boats, begun by Mr. Herreshoff in Gloriana, have been wonderfully developed in the greatest of all yachts, America's Defender.

MR. GOULD'S SHARE OF THE HONOR.

"Now that it has been definitely settled that the Defender will meet the Valkyrie in the races for the cup, it is proper to dwell on

[Continued from page 19]

COLUMBIA

COUNTESS OF DUFFERIN

the fact that Mr. George J. Gould's generosity in placing the old champion, the Vigilant, at the disposal of the Regatta Committee for use as a running mate to the new boat has been of the greatest benefit to the managers of the champion of 1895."

"If the exhilarating anticipation of a glorious struggle and a decisive victory shall be realized, no small part of the honor will be due to Mr. Gould. Without any expectation that the Vigilant would be chosen to defend the cup, but solely for the purpose of contributing to and establishing the Defender's superiority, he put his boat into competition at very large expense and has spared no effort to make her as useful as possible."

"Mr. Gould had the ballast in the old boat, over twenty tons in weight, transferred from her hold to her keel, under the eyes of an expert, Mr. Willard. In addition to this the Vigilant was strengthened internally and was fitted with sails said by good judges to be the finest ever spread off Sandy Hook."

"It is not an exaggeration to say that the Vigilant has been an indispensable factor in the preparation of the Defender. The magnitude of the service and the admirable spirit in which it has been rendered ought to be universally recognized and appreciated."

[*Defender and Valkyrie III Compared—Continued.*]

and has kept it on her. Some weeks ago I argued with the facts then on hand that Valkyrie III had more sail to wetted surface than the Defender. While the argument held good then, it does not now, because the Defender people—and very sensibly, too—have given their ship more sail. So when a mainboom is lengthened from 100 to between 105 and 107 feet, and the gaff from 61 to 64 feet, it is needless to say that such addition adds to the Defender's sail area; consequently what held good in argument before the change was made does not now. The conditions have been reversed in Defender's favor, for to-day she has more square feet of area to each foot of surface than the Valkyrie. This is again in favor of the Defender.

Thus we see Defender, with ten tons less displacement, with a greater sail area to wetted surface, pitted against the Valkyrie III, with greater displacement on the same driving power. I have turned over in my mind the two boats which will best help in comparison, so that the *Herald* readers may follow me through my argument. No two boats now afloat offer data for comparison of one against the other that the Defender and Valkyrie III do. All other boats are wider apart, some keel against centreboard, some ballast fin against keel. Different types of boats have heretofore raced for the America's cup. The only two boats of similar type, through which any sort of comparison can be made, are the 40-footers, the Gossoon and the life-boat the Minerva. The Gossoon, as every yachtsman knows, is a big, powerful 40-footer, with an enormous sail spread for her length. She is nearly three feet wider than the Minerva, has nearly a foot greater draught and has a much more powerful hull. She has a much larger sail plan than the Minerva, and she is between four and five tons more displacement than the Fife boat. Comparing the Gossoon with the Minerva on her spread of canvas the former has the much greater clothing. So we find in the Gossoon a bigger displacement boat, with more sail, more wetted surface, and on the same water line length, a larger and bigger boat to drive.

VALKYRIE III AND DEFENDER.

The Valkyrie is three feet wider than the Defender. She has also a foot more draught. Unlike the Gossoon, she has scarcely any advantage over the Defender in the matter of driving power. Never before in the history of cup racing were two yachts so close in the area of sail spread. The question, then, is, so far as the Defender and the Valkyrie go, which boat can be driven the faster with practically the same spread of canvas over them. Not only this; the Defender has ten tons less displacement and less feet of wetted surface. These all-important factors must be taken into consideration when passing upon the chances of one boat as against the other. How about driving the big hull of the Vigilant? might be asked.

The answer to this is, Vigilant to-day has about the same displacement as the Defender, but, with the former's new and larger sail spread, she has a greater per cent. of sail to wetted surface than either the Defender or Valkyrie. She has also less wetted surface than the 1895 boats. In clothing, the Valkyrie has hardly any advantage over the Defender. In wetted surface the Defender has less, so in displacement. On these three points, averaged up one against the other, the Defender has the advantage in theory and judged also by results.

[*Continued on page 23.*]

VOLUNTEER

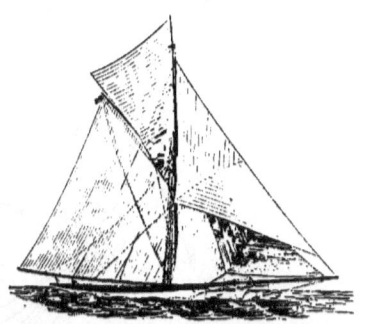

THE honors of victory in 1887 rested easy on General Paine and Edward Burgess. The coming Scotch yacht under the flag of the Royal Clyde Yacht Club was a "mystery" only until the Volunteer made a "show" of her. There are scores of the clans who are proud of the loss they suffered—proud even in defeat—for they were partisan Thistle men to the last, but the last came only too quickly for them, and the records of two races lost to Volunteer by over nineteen minutes in the first race and eleven in the second soon cleared the air of mystery.

Volunteer was a type of yacht entirely different from Mayflower, and equally distinctive as to shape as Defender differs from Vigilant. Volunteer was a magnificent boat on a beat. She pointed higher and fetched what she aimed at in a glorious style that put Thistle to the blush. Thistle, it is true, was able to run before the wind far faster than the Burgess craft, but on a reach or a beat she succumbed to Yankee smartness and prowess every time.

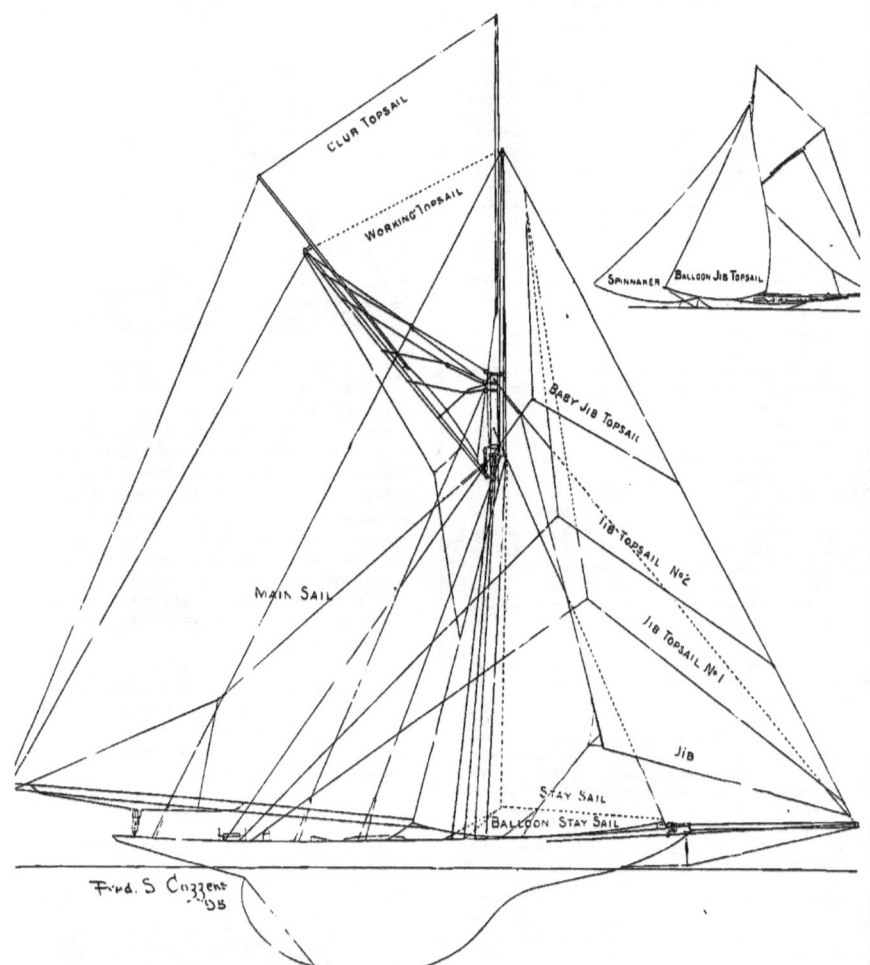

[*Defender and Valkyrie III Compared—Continued.*]

Should the Valkyrie III be sized up through the Britannia anyway?

What is there in Valkyrie that is similar to the Britannia? Absolutely nothing. So, in sizing up Valkyrie III with the Defender, the Vigilant is the boat, and none other.

Why? Because in the great essentials of her design she is more like the Vigilant than she is like the Britannia. It is plain and quite evident that Watson threw Thistle, Valkyrie II and Britannia overboard when he designed Valkyrie III. His boat shows this indisputably. Twenty-six feet two inches is quite close to Vigilant. Three feet wider than Britannia and six inches more added to this will give her beam over Valkyrie II.

How does Valkyrie III size up with the Vigilant, and, if improved, was it done in the same manner as the 1893 champion?

Hardly. The Vigilant was originally designed to float at eighty five feet water line. To this length all her water lines, calculations, ballast to displacement, sail area to wetted surface, were made. To-day she is below her actually designed lines, in fact she always was, and whatever she gains in water line length, she does it by being immersed by added weight. Her top body is not changed, neither is her entrance, consequently she has the same full water lines that she always had. Not so with the Valkyrie. As I have said many times, the Vigilant and only she is the bird Watson has leveled his gun on. What has he done to improve her?

First, he has taken all the data which he could find about Vigilant, and what was wanting about her he had somebody get for him, and with the knowledge of Vigilant's hull and sail spread, he has laid down on his draughting board not an immersed eighty-five footer, but a boat quite similar in general form to the Vigilant, but on paper 89 feet 6 inches on the water line, and at this she floats to-day. No one need be told that lengthening a boat's bow does not give her a sharper and cleaner entrance, and add to this the greater lengths of her two overhangs. The Valkyrie III has a sharper bow than Vigilant, on practically the same beam. Watson, then, has made his gain, be it what it may, by lengthening his boat in the design, so to speak. He knew from what he saw that Vigilant in 1893, when hard pressed, rolled out and threw a big side out to windward, and as one clever writer said, when she did it she drove one side through the water and the other through the air.

Watson has improved on Vigilant in another way, and this is in stepping the mast further forward. To-day there is less than half a foot difference between the stepping of the masts of Defender and Valkyrie III from the face of the stem at the load water line. Thus Valkyrie III and Defender stand about equal in having big mainsails for driving power. Look at the Vigilant and Valkyrie III under sail; there is a marked difference in the position of stepping the mast.

Again, take the sails. Sails cut like the Valkyrie's, with cloths running up and down, have stood gales of wind. There is some doubt about fore and aft cut sails standing such a test. Some people, and they are not amateurs either, predict in a hard blow they will split and go to pieces. So here again we have known tests against unknown ones.

In construction, too, the Valkyrie will stand it out just as long as the Defender, and longer, too. The Defender will be less hard on her canvas than Valkyrie III, consequently she needs heavier rigging. An old hand said to me at Erie Basin the other day : "Don't

[*Continued on page 36.*]

TIDES AND THEIR INFLUENCE ON THE RACES

AT 9.17 A.M., Saturday, September 7th, the old ocean will reach its high-water mark at Sandy Hook, and for an hour or an hour and a half will continue to run in through the Sandy Hook and Norton's Point gateway. About the time the yachts have started their great contest for international honors, the first of the ebb tide will have set out and formed a current due east, and during the next six hours that current will be carrying out a vast volume of water from the harbor of New York. This current changes its direction about one point an hour, and the last hour of the ebb tide finds the current running south-southeast.

Tuesday, September 10th, high water is expected at Sandy Hook at 11.23 A.M., but the flood will continue until probably 12 noon to 12.30 P.M., flowing about due north. Then the ebb tide will set out due east, and by one o'clock a strong current will be running to help or hinder the progress of the yachts; by two o'clock the direction of the current will change to east by south or east-southeast, and the same "swinging round the quadrant" will be repeated.

The hour for high water on Thursday, September 12th, is 12.24 P.M. ; add to this an hour or more for the time a flood continues and we find a current running north-northwest, north by west and then north along the Jersey coast for two hours and a half after the time for starting the yachts.

If a fourth race is necessary it will be on a flood tide, Saturday, September 14th. High water on that day is due at 2.28 P.M., and the race will be finished on a flood tide if there is a fair wind.

In the event of a fifth race on September 17th, there will be a tide just setting in from the eastward to aid or retard the speed of the yachts. If their course is laid to return from a mark southeast of the Lightship, the current coming in will help them.

In this description of the tides for these days no weather conditions are considered; high winds from the east or southeast will materially affect the flood, increasing its volume and prolonging the duration of high water; and similar winds from off shore will have a tendency to increase the time an ebb tide is flowing.

H. B. T.

"Farmer" Dunn Turns Yachtsman

To the Editor of the World:

The *World* requests from me a statement of weather conditions usually prevailing in September, the period covered by yacht racing. I have gone over the records of the weather bureau, and furnish you such facts as pertain to the matter. I cannot venture a prediction as to the probabilities, but your readers may draw their own inferences from the facts here set forth.

The month of September, generally speaking, is one of the pleasantest during the year, although it is one of three—July, August and September—in which West Indian hurricanes predominate, which occasionally ravage the Atlantic coast from Florida to Maine.

It is usually found that the winds to the south of the forty-fifth parallel are anti-cyclonic, while those to the north of that line are governed by the low pressure areas passing over Nova Scotia or Greenland, and assume more of the cyclonic nature.

During September storms occur less frequently over the interior of the country than during the colder months, and the average of severe ocean storms is less than the other months embraced in the cyclone period.

PREVAILING DIRECTION OF WIND.

1871	S. W.	1883	N. E.
1872	N. W.	1884	S.
1873	N. W.	1885	N. W.
1874	E.	1886	S.
1875	S. W.	1887	N. W.
1876	N. E.	1888	N. E.
1877	S. F.	1889	S. E.
1878	N. E.	1890	S.
1879	S. W.	1891	S.
1880	W.	1892	S. E.
1881	S. W.	1893	N. W.
1882	N.	1894	S. W.

The prevailing direction of the winds has been southwest to northwest.

It will be observed that while the prevailing winds are off shore, in quite a number of cases they have been from the more dangerous quarter or on shore, the direction depending entirely upon the position of areas of high or low pressure.

During this month the areas of high pressure composed of a bank of clear, compact air have a tendency to drift southeastward off the South Atlantic coast, in which event yachtsmen should look for winds blowing out from the high-pressure center, and wind from a southerly quarter may be expected as long as the center remains to the south of any given point. If the center should be to the north or west, then look for winds from that quarter.

The movement of winds from an area of high pressure is the same as the movement of the hands of a watch, and their duration depend entirely upon the extent and force of the area itself.

An area of low pressure is composed of warm, moist air, with the winds blowing inward to the center, or what is termed cyclonic winds. On the approach of an area of low pressure the winds along the coast blow from an easterly direction. Should the center of low pressure pass north of any given point then the winds would be from the south, blowing toward the center; should the center of low pressure pass to the south of you, then the winds would be from a northerly direction.

To determine the probable direction of wind during the racing season, yachtsmen or those interested may compute for themselves the probable direction of the wind by consulting the weather bureau chart, issued daily by the weather bureau in this city.

The force of the wind is probably a more important factor than the direction, and is much more difficult for the layman to predict. It depends entirely upon what is called the pressure gradient. For example, if there should be a difference in the reading of the barometer between the existing centers of high and low pressure of half an inch, within an area of one thousand miles a wind of from fifteen to twenty miles an hour might be expected. The greater the difference in pressure, the greater the force of the wind.

The average hourly velocity of wind throughout this neighborhood during September is nine miles an hour, and is a fresh sailing breeze. A brisk or whole-sail breeze should have a velocity of from fifteen to twenty miles an hour, which is no unusual occurrence, as may be seen by the following table of hourly maximum winds for the different years:

AVERAGE VELOCITY OF WIND, SEPTEMBER.

	Miles.		Miles.
1872	28	1884	27
1873	22	1885	37
1874	27	1886	27
1875	30	1887	30
1876	50	1888	25
1877	32	1889	48
1878	40	1890	25
1879	26	1891	28
1880	24	1892	36
1881	28	1893	30
1882	31	1894	36
1883	30		

A wind of from six to fifteen miles an hour is considered fresh; fifteen to twenty-nine, brisk; thirty to thirty-nine, high, and forty to fifty-nine, gale.

The majority of these months show velocities within the term "high," and three in which gales prevailed, the greatest being fifty miles an hour on September 17, 1876.

The pressure of wind per square foot on given sail surface may be of interest. Here are the figures:

Per Hour.		Pressure.		
5 miles		0.12 lb.	square foot	
10 "		0.50 "	"	"
15 "		1.12 "	"	"
20 "		2.00 "	"	"
25 "		3.12 "	"	"
30 "		4.50 "	"	"
35 "		6.12 "	"	"
40 "		8.00 "	"	"
45 "		10.12 "	"	"
50 "		12.50 "	"	"
75 "		28.12 "	"	"
100 "		50.00 "	"	"

The average number of clear days were 9; fair days, 12; cloudy days, 9.

The wind shows a slight increase in force during the latter part of the month.   E. B. Dunn.

International Racing in the Small Classes

THE rapidly growing interest in small craft, both racing and cruising, that has characterized the last few years of yachting abroad and at home, has this year resulted in the establishment by the Seawanhaka Corinthian Yacht Club of New York of an international challenge cup for perpetual competition between yachts of from 15-foot racing length (or one-half rating) up to 25-foot racing length (or two and one-half rating) under such restrictions as shall make the racing purely Corinthian. The announcement of the establishment of this trophy last March, and of a challenge from a well-known and successful English yachtsman, Mr. J. Arthur Brand, of the Minima Yacht Club, with a new boat, Spruce, the fourth of that name, and of a series of trial races in August to select a defending craft, brought together a fine fleet of seven of these mosquito boats at the club station, Oyster Bay, on August 26, 27 and 28, three races being sailed. The winning boat in all three races is a handsome little craft owned by Mr. C. J. Field, of the Indian Harbor Yacht Club, and built for him by the St. Lawrence River Skiff, Canoe and Steam Launch Co., of Clayton, N. Y., from the designs of Mr. W. P. Stephens, of the Seawanhaka Corinthian Yacht Club, an old canoeist and amateur designer as well as a writer on yachting.

The new boat, Ethelwynn, being designed especially for the conditions of these races, in which a crew of two is allowed, with a sail limit of but 225 to 250 feet, is not of the most recent bulb-fin type, but carries a centerboard of the least weight consistent with stiffness, 55 pounds. She is 23 feet 4 inches long on deck, 14 feet 6 inches on water line, and 6 feet beam, with a draught of hull of but 6 inches, with an extreme draught of 5 feet

when the long, narrow centerboard is lowered to its extreme point, the fore edge nearly vertical. The hull is a handsome piece of boat cabinet work, the inner skin of white cedar and the outer of mahogany, with union silk between.

One of the novel features of the boat is her rig, an improved leg-o'-mutton mainsail set on a hollow spar, with a very small jib. The whole boat is beautifully finished in hull and rig, all of the fittings being specially designed and made for her. In the three trial races she defeated a new Herreshoff centerboard boat especially built for the class, and also a sister boat to the celebrated Herreshoff bulb-fin Wee Winn, which has won so many victories in English waters.

The size of the English challenger is as yet unknown, other than that the total measurement will not exceed 15 feet racing length by the Seawanhaka rule. The boat and her owner will be in New York by September 8th, when the dates of the races will be arranged, sometime following the final races for the America's cup. The races will be sailed on Long Island Sound, off Oyster Bay, the winner of three out of a series of five holding the cup. While the American boat is at home, handled by a skillful crew, she has been in commission for less than a month, and neither of her crew have had any previous experience in racing in this type of boat. The challenger, on the other hand, is an old hand in the class, having sailed a great many races, while his boat, though new this season, has been sailed for some two months before starting from the other side. Whatever the result may be, the races are likely to lead to further additions to the class next year.

VALKYRIE III   DEFENDER

Two English Cup Challengers

CENESTA, 1885

THISTLE, 1887

[Defender and Valkyrie III Compared—Continued.]

you think the shrouds on the Defender lead too sharp, too much strain on them?'' Valkyrie has more spread, and does not feel the effect of her big mast as the Defender.

If Vigilant can carry her sail, and she can, better than ever, so can the Valkyrie III, which has a not much greater sail area.

VALKYRIE IS DANGEROUS.

If big-bodied Vigilant can be driven close to Defender in some races, why cannot Valkyrie III be driven just a little closer? The discussion of Valkyrie III and Defender is no new thing for me, because months ago I began work on approximate designs, which time has proved are in such close touch with the ships themselves that the data obtained from the figures have always led me to keep a weather eye on Valkyrie III, and see how this conundrum of Watson's would turn out. Not only this; such men as A. Cary Smith, Professor John L. Frisbee, instructor of naval architecture in the Boston schools, and Designer R. M. Woods, have talked the matter over with me, not in a selfish, narrow way, but out in the open, and every one of them opined that Valkyrie III would be a dangerous boat—yes, the boat most to be feared that ever came over here.

BRACE UP THE DEFENDER.

Defender can carry her sail; she has shown that. Those controlling her, should she need strengthening, should do it. Weight, when used to prevent disaster, pays doubly for itself. So, Mr. Iselin, if you think Defender needs any bracing, have it done. Do it anyway.

The Defender is the fastest all around boat ever seen under sail in this country. She has shown it in trial spins and in her racing.

In light winds she is fast; this she showed in her Sunday sail off Newport, when she drew away fast from the Vigilant. In moderate breezes she is fast, and all around at that.

The Defender is not a boat which is fast only on one point of sailing and falls off on the rest. She is fast, exceedingly so, to windward, fast in reaching, fast in running, no matter about wind and weather. I do not think she is at her best to-day; in fact, I know it. There are minutes in her yet, and the pity is there is not more time to develop her. She is easy in the sea, whether in light or heavy weather, and the boat which can beat the Vigilant as she is being raced to-day a minute a mile, as the Defender did in good wind off Newport, is a good one and there is no doubt of it. Take her last race off Sandy Hook and note her performance.

With the fear of carrying away her mast and not being driven after passing the Vigilant, but being nursed for nearly seven miles of the course, still she beat the Vigilant six minutes thirty-two seconds in ten knots. This means something, and on the above facts puts her between fifteen and twenty minutes faster than the Britannia over a thirty-mile course. Coming to one of the most vital questions, which is likely to play an all-important part in the result—the send away at the start, which ship will get the drop on the other? The send away may mean defeat at the line, and this brings me to the all-important matter of handling the ship, getting on and taking off sails—for seconds, not minutes, may decide the result.

A GREEN CREW.

On Defender there is a green crew, so to speak, from a racing standpoint. The men are all clever, bright, smart, intelligent chaps, full of Yankee pluck, which has been developed by hard and terrible

[Concluded on page 27.]

[Defender and Valkyrie III Compared—Concluded.]
service in fishing vessels. They are a willing, loyal set, true to
their ship, their owner and their flag. As a body, this is their first
year's racing. They have been together hardly five months, and
while to-day they are quite well up, yet there is room for doubt if
they can work together for the common end so well as men who
have been two, three, four and five years together, and these men
doing nothing but racing six months out of the year. They live on
yachts from boyhood, they know little else but racing, and Lord
Dunraven, no doubt, has picked the best men he can get. On the
question of handling, the Valkyrie's crew have certainly nothing to
fear in a try with the Defender's men.

As to sails, there again comes the question of practice and experience. On this side of the water there are not as many sails
made by hundreds as in Britain, and, like everything else, the more
work the sailmaker gets, the stronger he becomes. In material the
English duck makers seem more willing to experiment in yacht
canvas than they do on this side. Of late, however, the duck man-
ufacturers are looking into the matter more closely. The above
yarn tells its own tale; and now that I have discussed the ships as
best I could, always bearing in mind the great chances one takes of
walking overboard, and to carry out as best I can my assignment,
"Give your private opinion on the America's cup races":

Which will win?

In sea and wind?

Defender, sure.

In light winds and roll of sea, Defender.

In moderate breezes—Valkyrie's best chance—toss up. Defender has none the worst of it.

In light winds, smooth water, very close; sixes and sixes. Can't
call the turn.

Will Defender win three straight bouts?

Yes, if she has wind and sea, and everything stands. There
may be a break in light winds and smooth water.

In a sea and light winds the Defender should win out thrice
under these conditions.

The start will almost have as much to do with the result as the
weather.

If the Defender gets caught under the Valkyrie III's lee—well,
there will be some hair-singeing to get out.

Such are my opinions, given just like other people's, and like all
things that mortal man does, they may be wide of the mark.

To know about yacht naval architecture is not to talk about it,
because in the long run one, if he is sensible, will make up his
mind that he is dealing with conundrums, which nowadays cost
over $100,000 to try, and then may not turn out to be what you pay
for.

Anyway, if I do slip up, your readers will not be as bad off as
the syndicates which built both the Valkyrie and Defender. Watson
thinks—he opines—he's got the ship this time to do the trick. Herreshoff thinks and opines the same. Thousands of dollars are back-
ing up the opinions of both designers, and each thinks his boat will
win.

I can be changed by the actual result of the racing ; yes, just
as quick as Watson or Herreshoff.   A. G. McVey.

TEN YEARS OF INTERNATIONAL YACHT RACING

SEPTEMBER, 1885

GENESTA—Sir Richard Sutton

vs.

PURITAN—J. Malcolm Forbes

SEPTEMBER, 1886

GALATEA—Lieut. Henn, R.N.

vs.

MAYFLOWER—Gen. C. J. Paine

SEPTEMBER, 1887

THISTLE—James Bell

vs.

VOLUNTEER—Gen. C. J. Paine

OCTOBER, 1893

VALKYRIE—Earl of Dunraven

vs.

VIGILANT—C. Oliver Iselin *et al.*

SEPTEMBER, 1895

VALKYRIE III—Earl of Dunraven

vs.

DEFENDER—C. Oliver Iselin *et al.*

COMPARATIVE TABLE OF MEASUREMENTS

	Genesta	Puritan	Galatea	Mayflower	Thistle	Volunteer	Valkyrie	Vigilant
Length water line	81.00	81.00	87.00	85.70	85.00		86.82	85.00
Length over all							120.00	130.00
Beam	15.00	23.00	15.00	23.50	26.30		22.00	26.00
Draft	13.00	8.30	13.50	9.00			16.00	14.00
Displacement, tons	141.00	140.00	156.63	110.00	100.67			

Your Business
is
My Business

❦ ❦ ❦

I T IS my business to know something about your business if you want me to give you satisfactory results.

. . . Give me a few minutes some time before you place your Fall advertising, to run over the subject with you. My experience may serve to give you some points. I can tell you a lot about advertising—it will interest you; in this respect

❦ ❦ ❦

What's Mine
is
Yours

EDWARD Y. THORP
Publisher and Advertising Agent
CONSTABLE BUILDING
109 FIFTH AVENUE, ROOM 716

THE AMERICA'S CUP
"The Blue Ribbon of the Ocean."

IF the America's Cup were melted down and sold for old silver it would not bring more than $35. It cost nearly half a century ago $525. It was not, as is generally thought, a cup offered by the Queen, but was offered by the Royal Yacht Squadron, and given by the America's owners to the New York Yacht Club. Yet this little cup has cost the two nations quite $2,000,000. America has expended $900,000 of this to hold the trophy. When an international yacht race is on, the cup is exhibited for a day in Tiffany's, and occasionally on some high and solemn feast of the club it is brought out to grace the center of the table.

RECORD OF THE AMERICA'S CUP RACES.

CHALLENGERS AND DEFENDERS	OWNER	TON'GE	DATE	START h. m. s.	FINISH h. m. s.	TIME h. m. s.	COURSE
America....WINNER	G. L. Schuyler	170	Aug. 22, 1851	10 00 00	8 37 00	10 37 00	From Cowes around the Isle of Wight (Arrow second).
Arrow....		47	" 22, "	10 00 00	8 45 00	10 45 00	
Magic....WINNER	Franklin Osgood	93.3	" 8, 1870	10 56 00	3 58 54	4 58 21.2	N. Y. Y. C. Course (Cambria tenth).
Cambria....	J. Ashbury	227.6	" 8, 1871	11 26 00	4 00 57	4 37 26.9	
Columbia....WINNER	Franklin Osgood	220	Oct. 16, 1871	10 40 00	5 33 00	6 46 45	N. Y. Y. C. Course.
Livonia....	J. Ashbury	280	" 16, "	10 40 00	4 57 42	6 19 41	
Columbia....WINNER	Franklin Osgood	220	" 18, "	12 05 33½	3 07 15	3 07 41¾	20 miles to windward off Sandy Hook Lightship and return.
Livonia....	J. Ashbury	280	" 18, "	12 05 30½	3 10 10	3 18 15¾	
Columbia....WINNER	Franklin Osgood	220	" 19, "	1 25 00	3 18 05	4 02 25	N. Y. Y. C. Course (Columbia disabled.
Sappho....WINNER	W. P. Douglass	310	" 21, "	1 25 00	5 37 38	1 17 35	20 miles to windward off Sandy Hook Lightship and return.
Livonia....	J. Ashbury	280	" 21, "	12 11 00	5 44 24	5 39 02	
Sappho....WINNER	W. P. Douglass	310	" 23, "	12 12 52	6 17 30	6 09 23	20 miles to leeward off Sandy Hook Lightship and return.
Livonia....	J. Ashbury	280	" 23, "	12 15 12	5 59 05	4 16 17	
Madeleine....WINNER	J. S. Dickerson	151.49	Aug. 11, 1876	12 16 28	4 25 41	5 11 55	N. Y. Y. C. Course.
Countess of Dufferin....	C. Gifford	158.70	" 11, "	12 16 31	4 41 26	5 23 54	
Madeleine....WINNER	J. S. Dickerson	151.49	" 12, "	12 17 06	4 51 59	5 34 53	20 miles to windward off Sandy Hook Lightship and return.
Countess of Dufferin....	C. Gifford	158.70	" 12, "	12 17 24	5 37 11	7 18 46	
Mischief....WINNER	J. R. Busk	79.37	Nov. 9, 1881	12 17 58	8 03 58	7 46 00	N. Y. Y. C. Course.
Atalanta....	Alex. Cuthbert	84	" 9, "	11 14 50	3 31 59	4 16 09	
Mischief....WINNER	J. R. Busk	79.37	" 10, "	11 15 51	4 53 10	4 43 39¾	16 miles to leeward from Buoy 5 off Sandy Hook and return.
Atalanta....	Alex. Cuthbert	84	" 10, "	11 38 17	4 53 10	4 54 55	
Puritan....WINNER	J. Malcolm Forbes	140	Sept. 14, 1885	11 58 47	5 35 19	5 33 47	N. Y. Y. C. Course.
Genesta....	Sir Richard Sutton	80	" 14, "	10 22 00	4 38 05	6 06 05	
Puritan....WINNER	J. Malcolm Forbes	140	" 16, "	12 05 16	5 44 52	5 22 31	20 miles to leeward off Sandy Hook Lightship and return.
Genesta....	Sir Richard Sutton	80	" 16, "	12 06 01	4 10 39	5 03 11	
Mayflower....WINNER	Gen. C. J. Paine		" 9, 1886	10 56 12	1 32 53	5 26 41	N. Y. Y. C. Course.
Galatea....	Lieut. Henn, R. N.	90	" 9, "	10 56 11	1 45 22	5 38 43	
Mayflower....WINNER	Gen. C. J. Paine		" 11, "	11 22 40	6 12 40	6 49 10	20 miles to leeward off Sandy Hook Lightship and return.
Galatea....	Lieut. Henn, R. N.	90	" 11, "	11 24 10	6 42 58	7 18 09	
Volunteer....WINNER	Gen. C. J. Paine	209.8	" 27, 1887	12 31 38½	5 58 16½	5 33 18	N. Y. Y. C. Course.
Thistle....	James Bell	202.9	" 27, "	12 33 06	4 33 51	5 42 56¾	
Volunteer....WINNER	Gen. C. J. Paine	209.8	" 30, "	12 40 50½	4 93 12	5 34 45	20 miles to windward and return.
Thistle....	James Bell	202.9	" 30, "	10 40 21	3 30 47	4 05 17	
Vigilant....WINNER	C. Oliver Iselin et al.		Oct. 7, 1893	11 25 00	3 38 23	4 11 95	15 miles to windward and return.
Valkyrie....	Earl of Dunraven		" 7, "	11 25 00	3 50 01	4 25 01	Starting from Sandy Hook Lightship
Vigilant....WINNER	C. Oliver Iselin et al.		" 9, "	11 35 00	2 02 31	3 35 46	15 miles to windward and return.
Valkyrie....	Earl of Dunraven		" 9, "	11 35 00	2 30 31	3 24 39	Starting from Sandy Hook Lightship Equilateral triangle.
Vigilant....WINNER	C. Oliver Iselin et al.		" 13, "	12 27 00	2 51 39	3 25 19	15 miles to windward and return. Starting from Sandy Hook Lightship
Valkyrie....	Earl of Dunraven		" 13, "	12 27 00	2 53 52		Starting from Sandy Hook Lightship

THE MARINER'S COMPASS TRANSLATED
Anybody can "box" it

Johannis.

The King of

Johannis.

Table Water